GOLEM
A GIANT MADE OF MUD

BY MARK PODWAL

GREENWILLOW BOOKS, NEW YORK

Of the many versions of the golem legend in Jewish folklore, the most famous is the one about Rabbi Judah Loew ben Bezalel, who lived in Prague during the sixteenth century. History records that in 1592 Rabbi Loew, renowned as a brilliant scholar and mystic, was invited to an audience with Emperor Rudolf II. The emperor was fascinated with alchemy and the occult. This meeting served as the inspiration for many legends and stories, including the one in this book.

The sources I have used include:

Ripellino, Angelo Maria. *Magic Prague*. Berkeley: University of California Press, 1994.

Scholem, Gershom. *On the Kabbalah and Its Symbolism*. New York: Schocken Books, 1965.

Thieberger, Frederic. *The Great Rabbi Loew of Prague: His Life and Work and the Legend of the Golem*. London: Horovitz Publishing Company, 1955.

Wechsberg, Joseph. *Prague: The Mystical City*. New York: The Macmillan Company, 1971.

Gouache, colored pencils, and ink were used for the full-color art. The text type is Charter.

Printed in Hong Kong by Wing King Tong
First Edition 10 9 8 7 6 5 4 3 2 1

Library of Congress
Cataloging-in-Publication Data

Podwal, Mark (date)
Golem: a giant made of mud / retold by Mark Podwal.
    p.   cm.
Includes bibliographical references.
ISBN 0-688-13811-X (trade).
ISBN 0-688-13812-8 (lib. bdg.)
1. Golem—Juvenile literature.   [1. Golem.
2. Jews—Folklore.   3. Folklore.]   I. Title.
BM531.P63   1995
398.21'089'924—dc20
94-7865   CIP   AC

For Claudia

A long time ago, in the city of Prague, there lived an emperor who believed in all kinds of magic. But what he desired most was to find the secret of turning iron into gold.

Anyone who claimed he could make gold or who practiced magic was immediately granted an audience with the emperor. Alchemists, wizards, and magicians from every corner of the world flocked to Prague. The smoke of their efforts filled the skies with clouds.

Many alchemists and magicians were able to use the emperor's foolishness to earn fortunes for themselves. But those who deceived the emperor and were discovered were sentenced to death.

There was one sorcerer who not only claimed he could make gold but also announced that he could understand the language of birds. When the emperor realized that the sorcerer could do neither, he had him thrown from a window to see if he had learned from the birds the secret of flight.

Now, it happened that the emperor's evil advisors convinced him that the Jews of his kingdom possessed the formula for making gold and that the secret was recorded in one of their holy books.

The emperor ordered that the books be seized and a thorough search of them be made. When no formula was found, he decreed that the books be burned.

At that time in Prague there lived a great rabbi who, it was said, could perform miracles.

The rabbi went to the palace to plead with the emperor to save the holy books. On the way he was greeted by a crowd that pelted him with stones. But before the stones could reach their target, they turned into roses.

Suddenly the royal carriage appeared, and the people shouted at the rabbi to get out of the way. Covered with flowers, he remained standing right in the path of the carriage. Instead of running him down, the horses stopped on their own.

The emperor was so astonished that he permitted the rabbi to speak. Within hours the holy books were returned to the synagogue.

The emperor and the rabbi became friends, and the emperor promised to protect the Jews against their enemies. One day the emperor visited the rabbi's small, mud-caked house. He was accompanied by his chief astrologer, who wore a silver nose because his own had been cut off in a duel.

The rabbi's house, which had seemed so tiny and poor from the outside, was a palace within. Wherever they turned, new and magnificent rooms appeared. The rabbi had made the emperor feel comfortably at home.

In return the emperor invited the rabbi to see his collection of remarkable objects. There were iron nails said to have come from Noah's Ark, a horn from a unicorn, a giant's bone, a stone that grows, and a two-headed crocodile.

But what interested the rabbi most was a strange silver measuring spoon engraved with Hebrew letters. He recalled reading in *The Book of Creation* how a rabbi, long ago, had used such a spoon to create a golem, a figure made out of mud and then brought to life.

When the emperor heard the story, he was fascinated.

And so the rabbi continued with other stories. He told the emperor about a rabbi in Poland who also had created a golem from mud. The golem did the work that Jews were forbidden to do on the Sabbath. But once when this golem was asked to light a fire, the fire went out of control and the village burned down.

The rabbi related how still another rabbi and his students had recited the wrong prayer while trying to make a golem, and the earth had opened up and swallowed them.

When the rabbi prepared to go home, the emperor presented him with a gift. It was the silver measuring spoon engraved with Hebrew letters.

As time passed, the emperor, who had been cheated again and again by his alchemists and sorcerers, began to distrust everyone. Dressed in different disguises, he left the palace only at night. He spoke to no one but his pet lion, with whom, according to a fortune-teller, he shared the same horoscope.

People said the emperor was bewitched. They even whispered that he had lost his mind. The emperor's desk was piled high with neglected papers, and his evil advisors took control of the land.

It was a time of misery for the Jews, who could no longer depend on the emperor for protection. They were forced to live in a ghetto, a separate part of the city, in old, dilapidated houses crammed into gloomy alleyways. The ghetto was surrounded by a high wall, the gates of which were locked at night with heavy chains. There was only one sad garden, where the dead were buried.

One night the rabbi had a terrible dream. In his dream he
saw the ghetto being attacked and set on fire by a savage mob.
He awoke horrified.

For days the rabbi fasted, prayed, and studied the holy books.

Then one midnight, through a hidden passage beneath the city streets, the rabbi made his way to the river. With the help of a spoon that glittered in the moonlight, he molded a large figure from the mud of the shore.

How he brought the figure to life remains a mystery. Some say he simply placed a piece of parchment bearing God's name into its mouth. Others claim it was the Hebrew letters he inscribed on the golem's brow that gave it life.

The golem did not speak. It did not eat or drink. Both day and night it guarded the ghetto, wandering the maze of streets or watching over them from the rooftops.

With the exception of the rabbi, all who looked at the golem trembled inside. The rabbi hoped that the fear the golem instilled would prevent the disaster foreseen in his dream.

One day, as the sun was setting, the bells of every church in the city began to ring.

An angry mob armed with weapons and torches attacked the ghetto.

The golem rushed to the gates.

In its rage the golem grew larger and larger. Flames shot from its eyes and streaked across the sky. The terrified crowd ran in all directions.

Over the next few days the golem continued to grow. It became so enormous that the rabbi could no longer control it.

The golem caused ruin and destruction wherever it went. It tore out trees by their roots and tossed them at the moon. People were pulled apart as if they were dolls. Tall towers were flattened, and the golem wore the emperor's palace on top of its head like a crown.

The rabbi prayed that the golem would not bring about the

end of the world. And the slaughter and destruction stopped.

One afternoon, many years later, the rabbi's favorite granddaughter gave her grandfather a beautiful dark red rose she had picked. Hidden in the flower's fragrance was the Angel of Death, which flew out and took the rabbi away. A few years afterward the emperor died, one day after the death of his pet lion.

To this day nobody knows what became of the golem.

There are those who say a hand came down from heaven and removed the parchment that bore God's name from the golem's mouth, and the golem became a mountain of mud. The emperor's palace that once sat on its head now sat on the mountain top.

Others tell how the rabbi's prayers were answered in the form of an angel, who wiped the Hebrew letters from the golem's brow. The golem crumbled into countless pieces, which were used to rebuild the city it had destroyed.

And so today a golem might be anywhere, or everywhere, waiting to be brought back to life . . .

or perhaps all that remains are the stories.